All I Said Was...

Published in 2013 in Great Britain by
Barrington Stoke Ltd
18 Walker Street, Edinburgh, EH3 7LP

www.barringtonstoke.co.uk

This story was first published in a different form in
Wow! 366, Scholastic Children's Books, 2008

Text © 2008 Michael Morpurgo
Illustrations © Ross Collins

Individual ISBN 978-1-78112-297-6
Pack ISBN 978-1-78112-308-9

Not available separately

Printed in China by Leo

www.barringtonstoke.co.uk

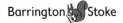

Michael Morpurgo
Illustrated by Ross Collins

All I Said Was...

I looked up from my book, and saw a bird at my window. All I said was, "Hi there, bird. You know what I'd like? I'd like to be you. I'd like to be able to fly off to any place I liked. That would be so good."

And he said, "That's fine with me. Just open the window and I'll come in. I'll lie on your bed and read a book. I've always wanted to read a book."

So in he hopped, and off I flew.

8

I flew out over the roof-tops, and down towards the sea. I was thinking, 'Wings are the best, wings are great. This flying lark is amazing. I want to be a bird all my life.'

But then, as I skimmed low over the beach, the gulls came after me. There was an army of them, all out to get me.

So I flew in over the land, over the rivers and fields.

And what happened?

The crows mobbed me.

So I landed in a field to hide.

And what happened?

A farmer chased me.

I don't know how I got
out of there, but I did.

I had had enough of all this by now. I was
thinking, 'Books are better, a whole lot
better. Next time I'll just read about being
a bird. I'll just imagine it. It'll be safer
that way. I'll live longer.'

I flew back to town and landed at my window.

And there he was, lying on my bed, reading my book.

Only, the odd thing was, he didn't look like a bird any more.

He looked like me!

19

Then I saw myself in the window.

I was still a bird!

I tapped on the window with my beak.

He looked up at me.

"Hi there, bird," he said. "You know what?
I'm reading a great story. It's all about
a boy like me who wants to be a bird like
you. So he does a swap, and becomes
a bird. Trouble is, it turns out he can't
change back. He's a bird for the rest of his
life. Isn't that a shame?"

Are you NUTS about stories?

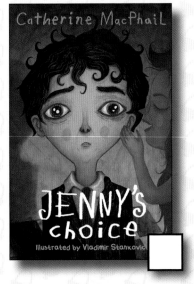

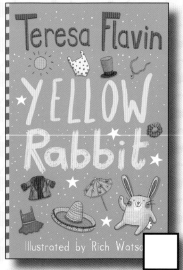

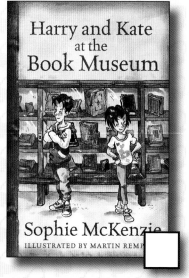

Read ALL the Acorns!